The
Shabbat Angels

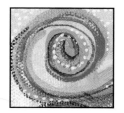

The Shabbat Angels

Maxine Segal Handelman

Illustrated by

Joani Keller Rothenberg

UAHC Press ✳ New York

For my mom, Arlene Segal, z'l,
who instilled in me the love of Shabbat,
and for Jacob, who shares it with me every week.

M S H

For Jeff, Leela, Ben Tamir, Maya, and Tal,
who bring joy to every Shabbat.

J K R

The music and words to *Shalom Aleichem* are from
The Complete Shireinu: 350 Fully Notated Jewish Songs,
published by Transcontinental Music (www. eTranscon.com).

This story was originally published in *Jewish Every Day:
The Complete Handbook for Early Childhood Teachers*
by Maxine Segal Handelman (Denver, CO: A.R.E. Publishing, Inc., 2000).

*T*here are many angels in this world who help God get every-thing done. Each angel has a special job. Two angels, Tov and Rah, are in charge of *Shabbat shalom*, Shabbat peace.

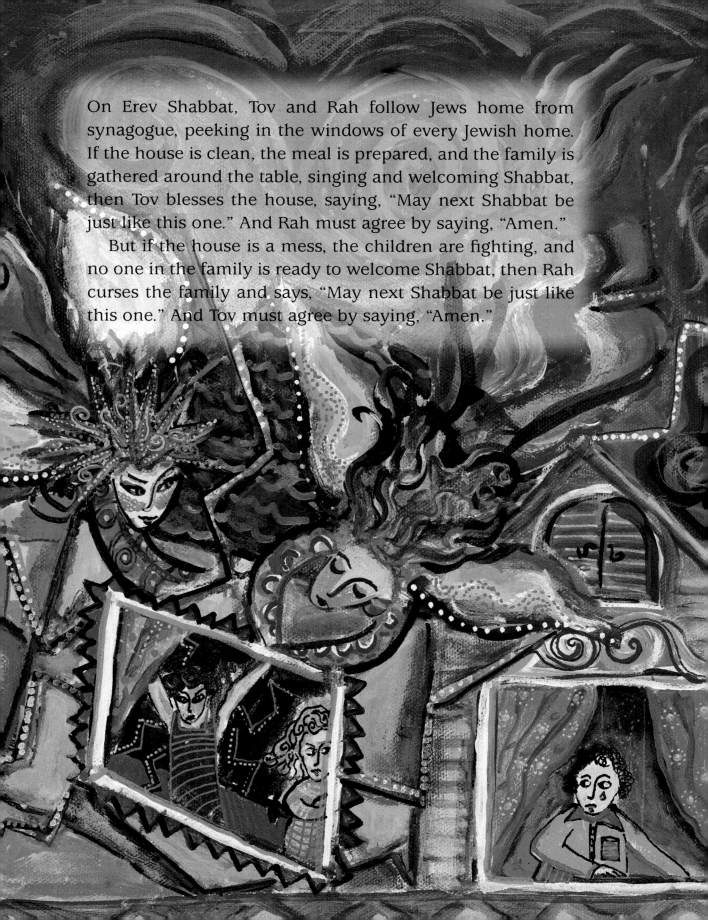

On Erev Shabbat, Tov and Rah follow Jews home from synagogue, peeking in the windows of every Jewish home. If the house is clean, the meal is prepared, and the family is gathered around the table, singing and welcoming Shabbat, then Tov blesses the house, saying, "May next Shabbat be just like this one." And Rah must agree by saying, "Amen."

But if the house is a mess, the children are fighting, and no one in the family is ready to welcome Shabbat, then Rah curses the family and says, "May next Shabbat be just like this one." And Tov must agree by saying, "Amen."

One day, Chaim Yonkel and his wife Esther had a big fight. Who knew what it was about? It was one of those little things that gets bigger and bigger all by itself. The fight lasted all week, and as Shabbat approached, Chaim Yonkel was still mad.

He was so mad that he neglected to buy flowers for Esther, as he usually did every Shabbat. Esther was still so mad that she decided not to make Chaim Yonkel's favorite kugel, the way she had every Shabbat for ten years.

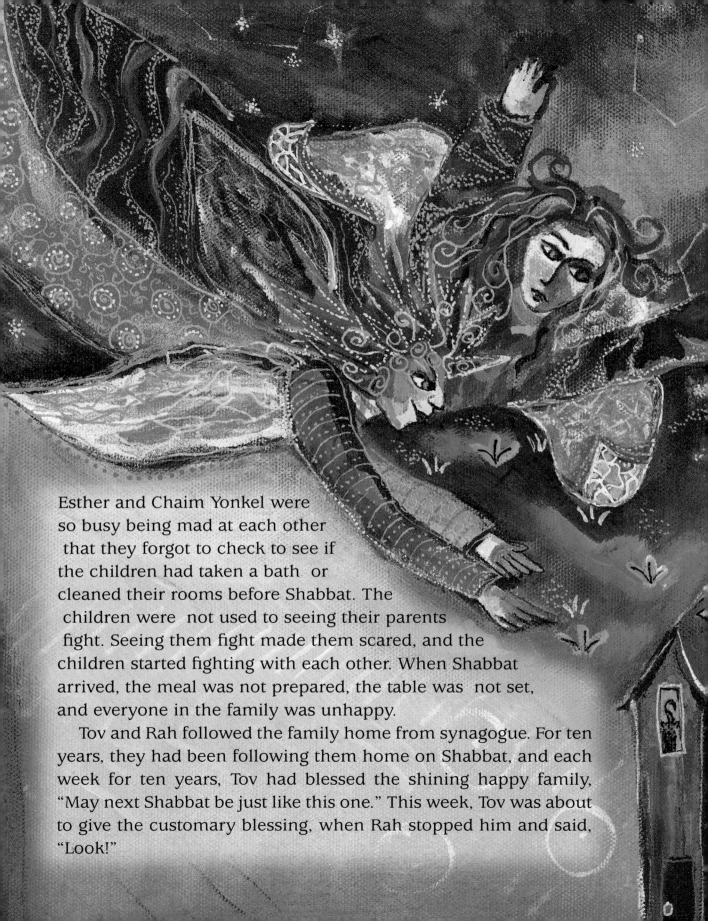

Esther and Chaim Yonkel were
so busy being mad at each other
that they forgot to check to see if
the children had taken a bath or
cleaned their rooms before Shabbat. The
children were not used to seeing their parents
fight. Seeing them fight made them scared, and the
children started fighting with each other. When Shabbat
arrived, the meal was not prepared, the table was not set,
and everyone in the family was unhappy.

Tov and Rah followed the family home from synagogue. For ten
years, they had been following them home on Shabbat, and each
week for ten years, Tov had blessed the shining happy family,
"May next Shabbat be just like this one." This week, Tov was about
to give the customary blessing, when Rah stopped him and said,
"Look!"

Rah pointed in the
window. Instead of seeing
candles burning and happy faces
singing, the two angels saw the
 youngest daughter pulling the hair of her
older sister, toys strewn all over the living room,
and angry sad faces on every member of the family.

"It's my turn this week!" declared Rah. "May next Shabbat be just like this one." Tov bowed his head and said, "Amen."

On Shabbat afternoon, Chaim Yonkel and Esther had some time to sit down and talk. When they realized that they couldn't remember what they had been fighting about, they laughed and hugged each other. "I'm sorry I made you upset," said Esther. "I'm sorry I made *you* upset," said Chaim Yonkel.

Chaim Yonkel and Esther gathered the children together and apologized to them for making their happy home such a sad place. By the end of Shabbat, everything was back to normal.

The week went by and everything was fine in the house. But as Shabbat approached, Rah's curse took effect. Chaim Yonkel became so busy at work that he forgot to buy flowers for Esther.

When Esther got home from work, she realized she didn't have all the ingredients for Chaim Yonkel's favorite kugel, but it was too late to go to the store before Shabbat began.

The children, having not cleaned their rooms the week before, found the mess had grown too large to finish cleaning before Shabbat.

When Tov and Rah followed the family home from the synagogue that night, Rah smiled triumphantly and said, "May next Shabbat be just like this one." And sadly Tov agreed, "Amen."

Chaim Yonkel, Esther, and the children were sad. What had happened to the *shalom* that had always filled their house on Shabbat?

When Shabbat was over, Chaim Yonkel, Esther and the children went to see the Rabbi. "Two weeks ago we were fighting," said Chaim Yonkel.

"Our Shabbat was ruined," said Esther.

"We stopped fighting, but this Shabbat wasn't any better," said the children.

"We want our happy Shabbat back!" cried the whole family.

The Rabbi listened closely. "Hmm," he said. "It seems that Rah, the bad Shabbat angel, has cursed your home. He saw you fighting on Shabbat, and he cursed your home that next Shabbat should be just like that one."

"Oh no!" cried Chaim Yonkel.

"What can we do to get our happy Shabbat back?" asked Esther.

The Rabbi thought for a long moment. "It will not be easy. You will *each* have to do your part," he said, looking into the eyes of each member of the family. "You must begin to prepare for next Shabbat now, even though it is an entire week away. Begin shopping, baking, cleaning today."

"Do something toward Shabbat each day this week, so it is never out of your minds or far from your hearts. If each one of you does his or her part, you might be able to beat Rah's curse."

On the way home, Esther stopped by the market and bought all the ingredients for Chaim Yonkel's favorite kugel. When the children got home, they started cleaning their rooms. Every day that week, Chaim Yonkel brought Esther a few flowers. As Shabbat approached, the family increased their preparations for Shabbat. Chaim Yonkel joined Esther in the kitchen, and together they baked a few new things they thought the family might like. Not only did the children clean their rooms, but each child went through her clothes and toys and picked out a few things to give to children without enough clothes or toys. On Friday, Chaim Yonkel made sure to leave work a little early, and he brought home the most beautiful bouquet of flowers he could find.

As the sun began to set, the family gathered together to light the Shabbat candles. The house was spotless, filled with the delicious smells of challah and the Shabbat meal, and each member of the family wore a big smile as they kissed and hugged and wished each other *"Shabbat Shalom!"*

When Tov and Rah peeked in the window, they heard the voices of the family joined together in song, "*Shalom aleichem, malachei hashareit*—Peace be to you, ministering angels...." Rah knew they were singing to him, telling him that they had beaten his curse.

Tov smiled his kind, good smile, and said, "May next Shabbat be just like this one." Rah bowed his head and agreed, "Amen."

Shalom Aleichem

Music: Samuel Goldfarb
Text: Liturgy

Lilting (♩ = 44)

V1&4 Em ... B7

1. Sha - lom a - lei - chem mal - a - chei ha - sha - reit
4. Tzeit - chem l' - sha - lom mal - a - chei ha - sha - lom

C B7 Em B7

mal - a - chei El - yon mi - me - lech mal - chei ham'-la - chim ha-

Am B7 Fine V2&3 G

ka - dosh ba - ruch Hu. 2. Bo - a - chem l' - sha - lom
(3.) chu - ni l' - sha - lom

D (B7) Em B7

mal - a - chei ha-sha - lom mal - a - chei El - yon mi - me - lech

Em (C) B7 Em D.C. (verse 4) al Fine

mal - chei ham'-la - chim ha - ka - dosh ba - ruch Hu. 3. Bar -

שָׁלוֹם עֲלֵיכֶם מַלְאֲכֵי הַשָּׁרֵת, מַלְאֲכֵי עֶלְיוֹן,
מִמֶּלֶךְ מַלְכֵי הַמְּלָכִים, הַקָּדוֹשׁ בָּרוּךְ הוּא.

Peace be to you, O ministering angels, messengers of the Most High, the supreme Ruler of rulers, the Holy One, blessed is God.

בּוֹאֲכֶם לְשָׁלוֹם מַלְאֲכֵי הַשָּׁלוֹם, מַלְאֲכֵי עֶלְיוֹן,
מִמֶּלֶךְ מַלְכֵי הַמְּלָכִים, הַקָּדוֹשׁ בָּרוּךְ הוּא.

Enter in peace, O messengers of the Most High, the supreme Ruler of rulers, the Holy One, blessed is God.

בָּרְכוּנִי לְשָׁלוֹם מַלְאֲכֵי הַשָּׁלוֹם, מַלְאֲכֵי עֶלְיוֹן,
מִמֶּלֶךְ מַלְכֵי הַמְּלָכִים, הַקָּדוֹשׁ בָּרוּךְ הוּא.

Bless me with peace, O messengers of the Most High, the supreme Ruler of rulers, the Holy One, blessed is God.

צֵאתְכֶם לְשָׁלוֹם מַלְאֲכֵי הַשָּׁלוֹם, מַלְאֲכֵי עֶלְיוֹן,
מִמֶּלֶךְ מַלְכֵי הַמְּלָכִים, הַקָּדוֹשׁ בָּרוּךְ הוּא.

Depart in peace, O messengers of the Most High, the supreme Ruler of rulers, the Holy One, blessed is God.

Author's Note:

The word for angels in Hebrew is *malachim*, literally "messengers." In the Talmud, Rabbi Yosei son of Rabbi Y'hudah tells the story of the two angels who follow each person home from synagogue on Shabbat. (*Shabbat* 119a). Tov is the angel of good, and Rah is the angel of evil. The *malachim* are spiritual forces sent by God. They do not inflict good or evil on us; they only reinforce and elevate the behavior we have chosen. Rabbi Yosei's story teaches us that God wants to help us, but God will only treat us the way we treat God. If we honor Shabbat with lit candles, a beautifully set table, and a clean house, then through the angels, God promises to assist us to repeat this performance the following week. If we do not honor Shabbat in these ways, then God has no choice but to assist us to continue the way we have chosen.

Thus, on Friday night, as we gather around the Shabbat table, in the presence of the shimmering candles, we sing the song *Shalom Aleichem* to welcome the ministering angels. It is if we are saying, "Come and see how beautifully we honor Shabbat. Bless us that it should be so next Shabbat as well!"